MINNESOTA VIKINGS

BY JOSH ANDERSON

Stride
An Imprint of The Child's World®
childsworld.com

The Child's World
childsworld.com

Published by The Child's World®
800-599-READ • www.childsworld.com

Photography Credits
Cover: © Leon Halip / Stringer / Getty Images; page 1: © Africa Studio / Shutterstock; page 3: © Grant Halverson / Stringer / Getty Images; page 5: © Hannah Foslien / Stringer / Getty Images; page 6: © Tony Duffy / Staff / Getty Images; page 9: © Hannah Foslien / Stringer / Getty Images; page 10: © Adam Bettcher / Stringer / Getty Images; page 11: © stevezmina1 / Getty Images; page 12: © David Berding / Stringer / Getty Images; page 12: © Gregory Shamus / Staff / Getty Images; page 13: © Larry French / Stringer / Getty Images; page 13: © Hannah Foslien / Stringer / Getty Images; page 14: © David Berding / Stringer / Getty Images; page 15: © Doug Pensinger / Staff / Getty Images; page 16: © DAVID GREENE / "Ai Wire Photo Service" / Newscom; page 16: © Rob Tringali / SportsChrome / Newscom; page 17: © Otto Greule Jr / Stringer / Getty Images; page 17: © AP Photo / Associated Press; page 18: © Tony Tomsic / SportsChrome / Newscom; page 18: © Donald Black/TNS / Newscom; page 19: © Christian Petersen / Staff / Getty Images; page 19: © Jamie Squire / Staff / Getty Images; page 20: © Jonathan Bachman / Stringer / Getty Images; page 20: © Hannah Foslien / Stringer / Getty Images; page 21: © David Berding / Stringer / Getty Images; page 21: © Kevin C. Cox / Staff / Getty Images; page 22: © "Ai Wire Photo Service" / Newscom; page 23: © Jeff Gross / Staff / Getty Images; page 23: © stevezmina1 / Getty Images; page 25: © Star Tribune file photo/TNS / Newscom; page 26: © Bruce Bisping/ZUMA Press / Newscom; page 29: © Scott Halleran / Staff / Getty Images

ISBN Information
9781503857865 (Reinforced Library Binding)
9781503860575 (Portable Document Format)
9781503861930 (Online Multi-user eBook)
9781503863293 (Electronic Publication)

LCCN 2021952674

Printed in the United States of America

BRINGING THE WORLD TO YOUNG READERS 1968

TABLE OF CONTENTS

GO VIKINGS!

The Minnesota Vikings compete in the National Football **League's** (NFL's) National Football Conference (NFC). They play in the NFC North **division**, along with the Chicago Bears, Detroit Lions, and Green Bay Packers. The rivalries in the NFC North are some of the oldest and fiercest in the entire NFL. The Vikings have made the **playoffs** 30 times and played in four **Super Bowls**, but they have yet to win the big game. Fans hope that will change soon! Let's learn more about the Vikings!

NFC NORTH DIVISION

Chicago Bears

Detroit Lions

Green Bay Packers

Minnesota Vikings

WIDE RECEIVER JUSTIN JEFFERSON JOINED THE VIKINGS IN 2020 AFTER WINNING A NATIONAL CHAMPIONSHIP WITH LOUISIANA STATE UNIVERSITY.

JORDAN
83

BECOMING THE VIKINGS

The Vikings began play in the NFL as an **expansion team** in 1961. The team is named after the Vikings of ancient Scandinavia, an area in Northern Europe. The name made sense because there are a lot of people of Scandinavian descent in the state of Minnesota. While the Vikings have never won the Super Bowl, they played in the big game four times from 1969 to 1976. They've also made it to the NFC Championship Game six other times.

QUARTERBACK WADE WILSON PLAYED IN 76 GAMES FOR THE VIKINGS FROM 1981 TO 1991.

BY THE NUMBERS

The Vikings have played in **FOUR** Super Bowls.

20
division titles for the Vikings

556
points scored by the team in 1998—a Vikings record!

13
wins for the Vikings in 2017

THE VIKINGS MADE IT TO THE PLAYOFFS THREE TIMES BETWEEN 2015 AND 2019.

FANS ENJOY THE HIGH-TECH PLAYER INTRODUCTIONS AT U.S. BANK STADIUM.

GAME DAY

The Vikings shared their original home, Metropolitan **Stadium**, with the Minnesota Twins baseball team from 1961 to 1981. After that, both the Vikings and the Twins moved into the Hubert H. Humphrey Metrodome. Since 2016, they've played in their current home, U.S. Bank Stadium. On a normal Vikings game day, U.S. Bank Stadium holds nearly 67,000 football fans. In 2018, the building hosted the Philadelphia Eagles' 41–33 victory over the New England Patriots in Super Bowl 52.

We're Famous!

In addition to their eye for football talent, the Vikings are good at spotting professional wrestling talent as well! Brock Lesnar and Roman Reigns are two of the top performers in World Wrestling Entertainment (WWE). They both played football before their pro wrestling days. Lesnar joined the Vikings in the preseason in 2004, but he was cut before the regular season. Reigns was signed to the Vikings in 2007, but he never got a chance to play in any games for the team.

UNIFORM

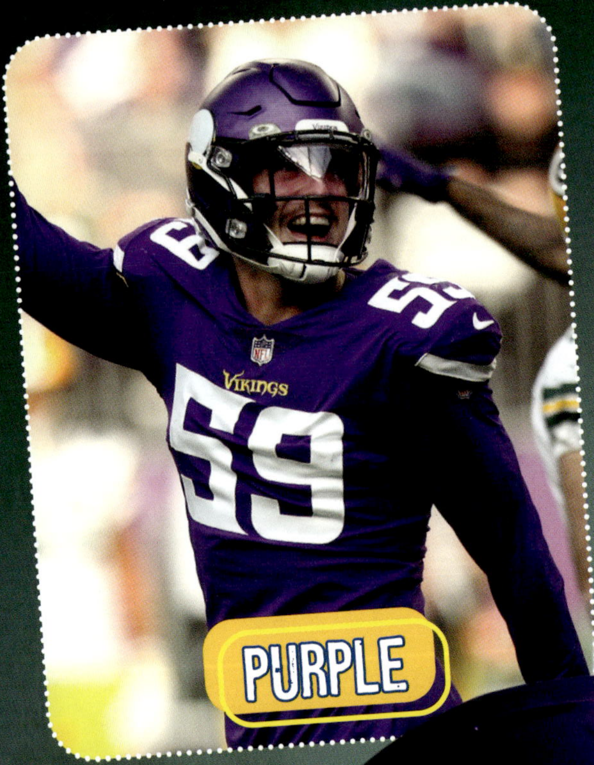

Truly Weird

With just over two minutes left to play in a 2013 game, the Vikings led the Baltimore Ravens 12–7. But a **touchdown** pass by Ravens quarterback Joe Flacco gave Baltimore the lead. Amazingly, the lead would change five times in the final two minutes and five seconds. With only four seconds left, the Ravens scored a touchdown and took the lead from the Vikings for good, 29–26. The teams combined for 36 points in the final minutes of the game!

Alternate Jersey

Sometimes teams wear an alternate jersey that is different from their home and away jerseys. It might be a bright color or have a unique theme. The Vikings wore uniforms with purple jerseys and pants for a game against the Dallas Cowboys in 2020. The new look proved unlucky, though. The Vikings lost the game.

SOME VIKINGS FANS GO ALL OUT. A GROUP OF PARTICULARLY PASSIONATE FANS CALL THEMSELVES THE "VIKING WORLD ORDER."

TEAM SPIRIT

Going to a game at U.S. Bank Stadium can be a lot of fun! In Norse mythology, an instrument called the Gjallarhorn was blown to announce the arrival of the gods. So every Vikings home game starts with a ceremonial blowing of the Gjallarhorn by either a former player or other honorary Viking. This gets the crowd fired up and ready for the game.

The Minnesota Vikings Cheerleaders entertain fans during breaks in the action and at halftime. They're joined by Viktor the Viking, a huge costumed Viking character. He's been rooting for the team since 2007.

VIKTOR

HEROES OF HISTORY

Cris Carter

Wide Receiver | 1990–2001

Carter ranks fourth all-time with 130 receiving touchdowns. He also ranks 13th all-time with 13,899 receiving yards. Carter led the league in touchdown catches three times as a Viking. He was chosen for the **Pro Bowl** eight times. In 2013, he was inducted into the Pro Football **Hall of Fame**.

Randy Moss

Wide Receiver | 1998–2004; 2010

Moss was nicknamed "the Freak" for his incredible combination of size and speed. Moss ranks second all-time with 156 receiving touchdowns. He also ranks fourth all-time with 15,292 receiving yards. During his time with the Vikings, Moss led the league in touchdown catches three times. He is a member of the Pro Football Hall of Fame.

Adrian Peterson

Running Back | 2007–2016

Peterson ranks fourth all-time with 120 rushing touchdowns and fifth all-time with 14,918 yards. As a Viking, Peterson led the NFL in rushing three times. In 2012, he won the NFL's **Most Valuable Player** (MVP) Award after he rushed for 2,097 yards and 12 touchdowns. He's been selected for the Pro Bowl seven times.

The "Purple People Eaters"

Defensive Linemen | 1968–1976

The Vikings' talented defensive line of the late 1960s and 1970s were nicknamed the "Purple People Eaters." Anchored by Hall of Famers Alan Page and Carl Eller, the group helped the Vikings advance to the Super Bowl four times. During their era, the Vikings finished in the top three for fewest points allowed in a season seven times.

The Vikings defeat the Dallas Cowboys 27–10 in the NFC Championship and advance to their second Super Bowl.

With a chance to advance to their fourth Super Bowl in eight years, the Vikings defeat the Los Angeles Rams in the NFC Championship Game 24–13.

BIG DAYS

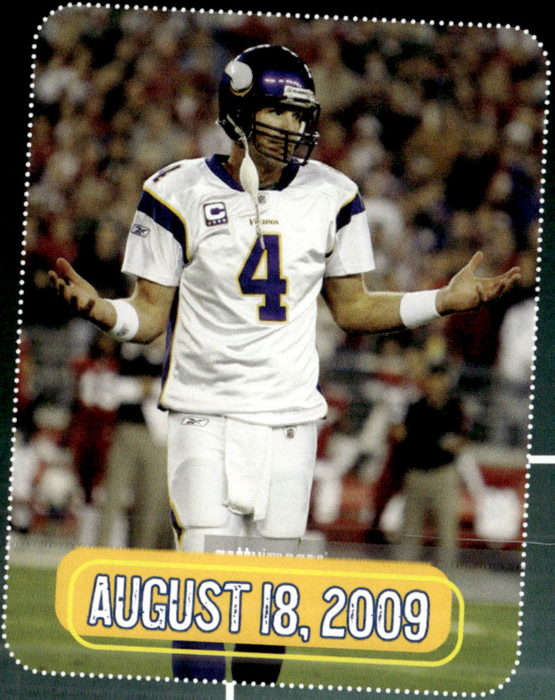

After leading the Green Bay Packers for 16 seasons, legendary quarterback Brett Favre signs on to play for the Vikings.

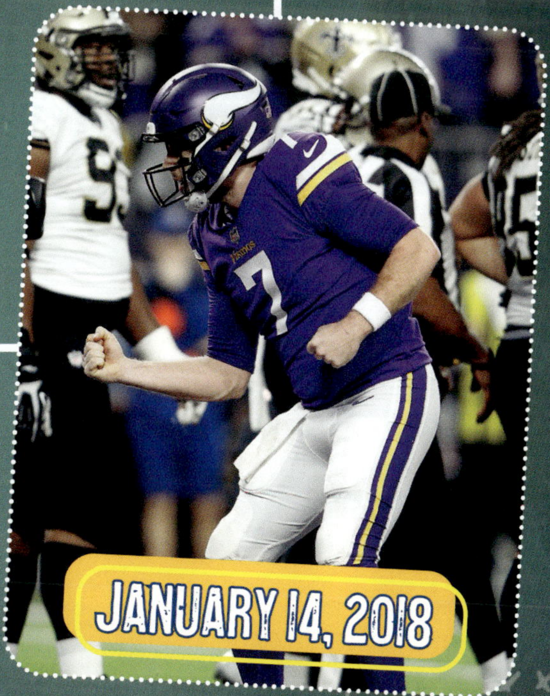

The Vikings defeat the New Orleans Saints 29–24 in a playoff game to advance to their first NFC Championship Game since 2009.

MODERN-DAY MARVELS

Dalvin Cook

Running Back | Debut: 2017

Cook is the all-time leading rusher in Florida State University history. As a pro, Cook rushed for more than 1,000 yards in three-straight seasons from 2019 to 2021. In 2020, Cook finished second in rushing yards with 1,557 and rushing touchdowns with 16. He earned Pro Bowl honors following the 2019, 2020, and 2021 seasons.

Kirk Cousins

Quarterback | Debut: 2018

Before coming to Minnesota, Cousins played six seasons for the Washington Commanders. In four years with the Vikings, Cousins passed for 124 touchdowns and only 36 interceptions. During that time, he led the team to a record of 33–29–1. In his career, Cousins has been selected for two Pro Bowls.

Justin Jefferson

Wide Receiver | Debut: 2020

Jefferson helped lead Louisiana State University to the 2019 college football National Championship. In 2020, the Vikings selected him in the first round of the NFL Draft. Jefferson totaled 3,016 receiving yards and 17 touchdowns in his first two seasons. He was chosen for the 2020 and 2021 Pro Bowls.

Adam Thielen

Wide Receiver | Debut: 2014

Thielen is the only player in NFL history to start a season with eight games in a row with 100 or more receiving yards. He finished with more than 1,000 receiving yards in 2017 and 2018. In 2020, he ranked third in the NFL with 14 touchdown catches. Thielen has been chosen for the Pro Bowl twice.

QUARTERBACK FRAN TARKENTON WAS CHOSEN FOR THE PRO BOWL NINE TIMES DURING HIS CAREER.

THE GOAT

GREATEST OF ALL TIME

FRAN TARKENTON

Tarkenton ranks 11th all-time with 342 passing touchdowns. He also ranks 14th all-time with 47,003 passing yards. Tarkenton ranked in the top ten in the NFL for passing yards 17 times. He led the Vikings to the Super Bowl three different seasons. In 1975, Tarkenton was selected as the NFL's MVP. And in 1986, he was inducted into the Pro Football Hall of Fame.

FAN FAVORITE

Daunte Culpepper–Quarterback

1999–2005

Culpepper earned the hearts of fans with his resourcefulness as a quarterback. He could dominate a game with his strong arm, but he also used his legs to control the action. In addition to ranking third in team history with 20,162 passing yards, he also rushed for 2,476 yards as a Viking.

THE BIG GAME

JANUARY 4, 1970 – NFL CHAMPIONSHIP GAME

The Vikings finished the 1969 season with a 12–2 record. That was the best record in the NFL that year. Their playoff game against the Cleveland Browns would decide who would face the Kansas City Chiefs in Super Bowl 4. The Vikings had never played in the big game before. While the Browns had a powerful offense, the Vikings had given up the fewest points in the NFL that season. The Vikings defense continued its strong play in the playoffs. They held the Browns without any points until the fourth quarter. The Vikings won 27–7.

KICKER FRED COX SPENT ALL 15 SEASONS OF HIS PROFESSIONAL FOOTBALL CAREER WITH THE VIKINGS.

BUD GRANT LED THE VIKINGS TO 158 REGULAR SEASON VICTORIES FROM 1967 TO 1985.

AMAZING FEATS

4,717 Passing Yards

In 2004 by QUARTERBACK Daunte Culpepper

2,097 Rushing Yards

In 2012 by RUNNING BACK Adrian Peterson

122 Catches

In 1994 & 1995 By RUNNING BACK Cris Carter

17 Receiving Touchdowns

In 2003 by WIDE RECEIVER Randy Moss

ALL-TIME BEST

PASSING YARDS

Fran Tarkenton
33,098

Tommy Kramer
24,775

Daunte Culpepper
20,162

RUSHING YARDS

Adrian Peterson
11,747

Robert Smith
6,818

Chuck Foreman
5,887

RECEIVING YARDS

Cris Carter
12,383

Randy Moss
9,316

Anthony Carter
7,636

SACKS*

Carl Eller
130.5

Jim Marshall
128

John Randle
114

SCORING

Fred Cox
1,365

Cris Carter
670

Ryan Longwell
633

INTERCEPTIONS

Paul Krause
53

Bobby Bryant
51

Ed Sharockman
40

*unofficial before 1982

HALL OF FAME DEFENSIVE LINEMAN JOHN RANDLE LED THE NFL WITH 15.5 SACKS IN 1997.

GLOSSARY

division (dih-VIZSH-un): a group of teams within the NFL that play each other more frequently and compete for the best record

expansion team (ek-SPAN-shun TEEM): a new team added to the league

Hall of Fame (HAHL of FAYM): a museum in Canton, Ohio, that honors the best players in NFL history

league (LEEG): an organization of sports teams that compete against each other

Most Valuable Player (MOHST VAL-yuh-bul PLAY-uhr): a yearly award given to the top player in the NFL

playoffs (PLAY-ahfs): a series of games after the regular season that decides which two teams play in the Super Bowl

Pro Bowl (PRO BOWL): the NFL's All-Star game in which the best players in the league compete

stadium (STAY-dee-uhm): a building where teams play, with a field and seats for fans

Super Bowl (SOO-puhr BOWL): the championship game of the NFL, played between the winners of the American Football Conference (AFC) and NFC

touchdown (TUTCH-down): a play in which the ball is brought into the other team's end zone, resulting in six points

FIND OUT MORE

IN THE LIBRARY

Bulgar, Beth and Mark Bechtel. *My First Book of Football.* New York, NY: Time Inc. Books, 2015.

Jacobs, Greg. *The Everything Kids' Football Book, 7th Edition*. Avon, MA: Adams Media, 2021.

Scarpati, Kevin. *Minnesota Vikings*. New York, NY: AV2, 2020.

Sports Illustrated Kids. *The Greatest Football Teams of All Time*. New York, NY: Time Inc. Books, 2018.

ON THE WEB

Visit our website for links about the Minnesota Vikings:
childsworld.com/links

Note to parents, teachers, and librarians: We routinely verify our web links to make sure they are safe and active sites. Encourage your readers to check them out!

INDEX

ABOUT THE AUTHOR

Josh Anderson has published over 50 books for children and young adults. His two boys are the greatest joys in his life. Hobbies include coaching his sons in youth basketball, no-holds-barred games of Apples to Apples, and taking long family walks. His favorite NFL team is a secret he'll never share!